The Waterland Massacre:
An Electrifying Thriller of Suspense and Mystery

Aiden Ziff

"I'm not going to hurt you Wendy, I'm just going to rip your fucking head off." –**Jack Torrance**

    -The Shining (1980)

Foreword

Since 1925 in Waterland Texas people have been mysteriously disappearing, Waterland is located between several natural reserves immersed in a mountain range of valleys and forests with difficult access... there are also several abandoned mines from the 1900s.

Unfortunately, the bodies have never been found, only the testimony of the relatives has remained as evidence, but as far as the government is concerned, it has not entered into a serious investigation into the roads and gaps of that great extension of kilometers despite the countless testimonials that someone has been murdering people near the town of Wilstermann . Some suspect that there is a serial killer in those woods, others simply point to the dangerous rugged geography of the area that the entire forested strip counts... But in 2006 four surviving children of that killer managed to tell me the truth of what they saw. His parents were brutally murdered as well as a group of policemen. The bodies were never found except for an intact patrol car with no trace of blood. Who really is or who are the ones behind the disappearance of dozens of people a year in this area? Immerse yourself in this horror story that happened in 2006, and if for some reason you go to this region of Texas and a book called *'sawtooth or don't buy me'* ever arrives at your house ; it is better that you run away, because it is the sign that this psychopath or murderer is close and coming for you.

The local media have not talked much about this, perhaps so as not to alarm the population, and they only limit themselves to passing information vaguely. But now you will know what is really hidden in the mountains of Waterland .

Index _

Part 1

Town of Wilstermann Texas 2004, population 1290 inhabitants.

Thirty-three-year-old Milly Brown was a single mother who worked as a teacher at the rural school in that town. He had two girls; Laurel is seven and Anita is ten, as well as a beautiful and spacious house at the edge of the beginning of the dry forest. The town was immersed between large natural reserves of oak and noble forest and wooded areas. It also had strips with pronounced canyons and grasslands. Very quiet and beautiful place to live.

On the morning of October 3, the postal service left a package at the Browns' house. As usual, she left work at 7:00 in the morning, so she wouldn't see him until the afternoon. Once back, the first thing that was said when he opened the locker:

- Whoa! I got quite a bit of mail today, and that weird package at the bottom, what the hell is it? mmm I see they were wrong, the address is mine, but as far as I know I didn't buy any books online and less horror as it seems, I hate that genre. Well, I think I'll give it to one of my students.

After a while the book lay in the kitchen on one side of the marble table. The seven-year-old girl named Laurel asked her permission to read it.

— Mom, mom, and that book that has that ugly drawing of terror? Who gave it to you?

— Surely someone made a mistake honey and put our address and well it arrived, but tomorrow I'll give it away, I don't like horror books for you. she said as she heated up slices of pizza on a grill.

But can I open it?

— mmm , since you insist,

"Thank you mommy," Laurel recited.

A few minutes passed and the girl began to leaf through the book, everyone's big mistake.

- And what is it? - inquired the mother while washing some dishes. — go ahead show me how good you are at reading love.

"Okay mommy, but...

— What are you waiting for Laurel, while the pizza is heating up, read me a page, but now! because we'll start eating in a moment. he insisted again.

The girl began to read something like: "the footsteps that come behind you are real, don't think you're dreaming, the faceless man is coming because he doesn't really wear a mask, run boy run, I'll see you soon in the forest. Run, run, there is no way out of my area, once you cross these letters it will be impossible to see your mommy again, do you know why girl? because all your place belongs to me, including you, so I want you to go outside tomorrow and you will see that you will no longer be in your neighborhood" — .

Hearing such a story Emily was alarmed and uttered:

- What the hell! have Anita give it to me, what are those hoaxes.

When the mother held the book, she realized that only that fragment contained the third page and the rest of the pages were empty and looked old. Then he exclaimed:

— What a good joke, surely it is cheap publicity, the strange thing is that how do they know that there are girls? Yes, I see!

It's probably an internet advertising company, but how did they know that we live only women? maybe it's some propaganda, lately they bother a lot. It is the bad thing about accepting the conditions on any internet page; They steal your data and sell it to wretches. Well, I was thinking of giving it away, but I see that it has no valuable content. Anita takes the book to the trash can and come eat.

The girl did as her mother had told her, when she put the book inside the basket, on the other side of the street a strange man dressed as a reaper was motionless looking at her. His attire was strange, in that place of population mostly retirees, something like this would never be seen. He wore a straw hat that did not allow his face to be seen, and old and worn clothing. When the girl turned to enter the house, and when she turned again, the strange subject had disappeared. But he did not miss the opportunity to tell his mother.

— Mom, you won't believe what I just saw; a guy dressed weird in front of the Hamilton house and he gave me ugly looks.

— It's not Halloween yet honey, I think that guy in this heat is going to be random.

— I don't know , but that guy was looking at me I guess under his mask.

— Honey, it's okay, maybe he wanted to scare you, but princesses shouldn't be scared with silly costumes. Come on! Come eat your pizza is already getting cold.

Two weeks have passed since that incident. And the day for the walk with the Morgans had arrived. Mr. Jean Morgan was a forty-year-old ex-military man who, like Emily, was a single father of two boys ages sixteen and sixteen, and had only been in the neighborhood for a short time, no more than three months.

Although he was a native of there, and had gotten along very well with Mrs. Brown who even went on regular family outings since she taught both children. Also, with him lived his thirty-seven brother Thomas, a bohemian and party guy who didn't care about life, but who was wealthy since he had received a fortune from his late wife of seventy years.

It was 8 am when the Morgans arrived at the Brown residence in their fifteen-passenger Express Van.

"I see you're ready," Jean Morgan asked as she got out of the car to help him load the things.

"Yes, we're ready, " Emily replied instantly, greeting him with a kiss.

— Give me those five Laurel... come on, don't make that face, Anita, it will be an incredible walk, you'll see. My boys are still sleeping in there, my brother you know Emily and his bad manners. Jean yelled.

— Well, I'll take these things up to leave if not, we won't get to the lake reserve in time. — I see that Jonathan of ten is the same as Anita, they don't like to go for a walk,

- Emily nodded and murmured - adolescence and its hormones.

— I remember that age Emi like it was yesterday... Well, if you don't forget anything, it's time to put this baby on the road — Jean said as she started the engine.

Part 2

The lake was about thirty kilometers from the town of Wilstermann , immersed in the mountains and deep in the forest.

- Do you have the map? asked his brother.

"Of course, how many times we went to that place when we were young, you almost forgot, if we came recently, " answered Tom.

— The hills are old, I still feel like a young man, my memory remembers little by little. It will be a good weekend for everyone - Jean affirmed while looking at the sunny sky on the horizon.

— I wanted it a lot — Emy said, — since you invited me Jean two weeks ago I hadn't decided, but I see that we were roasting in the town and it would be great to swim in that lake I told myself. The truth is that I have lived in that place for five years and I did not know that there was a lake near here, well what I mean is that a stream runs behind the dry forest, but I did not know that there was a small lagoon far below and surely that stream goes there . I hope you have made me understand...

— What happens is that it is a private area, in fact, it has no owner, but since my grandfather was a close friend of the owner who died many years ago, we practically took it as our own, although in legal terms we are not, but it is That's why no one enters, it's inside some fields that very few people know exist.

- Oh! what little guard they had.

— It was a bit hilly, but last week Tom and I were cleaning up a bit where the house is facing the lake. How we were going to invite you and bring the children I wanted it to be ideal.

" Dad, are we going to get there yet?" Jonathan asked, while making a lazy face.

"I'm talking to the lady, don't be rude," Jean scolded him.

After a while the road ended and two gaps of unpaved roads began, Mrs. Brown asked.

— This place is beautiful, and finally, which path leads to the place where we are going?

"On the right side," Tom yelled from the last seat.

- That is right, brother,

"And where is the other one going?" she replied.

— The other one doesn't go anywhere... I think it's about four kilometers of dirt road and at the end is the beginning of an old mine.

— Oh! okay, I understand, so the mine, the water, the stream, right?

— Correct, about a hundred years ago that mine was closed for unknown reasons, the owner of all this place was called Milton Crower , and well he died mysteriously, then my grandfather was the one who fenced off this entire region again, more than anything so that nobody invaded it, and since we were children at that time we came to play all over this place, and time took us away from this town... and you know the rest, I've known you for three months.

— What a beautiful story Jean, you hadn't told me.

"You should ask me more questions.

"Ok sir, I promise to make you more," he said as he laughed.

Jean began to drive into the gap in the dirt road that led to the lake house. The whole road seemed very rugged and lonely and quite neglected.

"Mom, Mom, there are crows in the tree there," Laurel yelled from the backseat as she stuck her head out of the car a little.

— I already looked at them, don't stick your head out you can hit yourself with a branch.

"They're eating a dead deer," Tom asserted to the sound of his tobacco-chewing molars.

— Don't scare them Tom, don't fuck. We have enough with your vices.

- Goes! Now, children watch terrifying things on the internet, that does not cause fear or a fagot. Believe me.

After a while the car was knocked over by a log in the middle of the road that Jean did not look at.

"What the hell was that, you look like a babe driving," Tom yelled as his craft beer spilled down his fly.

- Good heavens! I hope the gas tank didn't screw up, because it did feel pretty strong the blow, they are all well, right? Jean asked.

— Yes, they all murmured in the back.

— Brother, give it a review, you know mechanics.

reluctantly got out and checked that everything was fine, and luckily for everyone it had only been the scare. And the bumper somewhat dented.

— We're in luck, it was just the crash, it didn't damage anything, but be more careful I don't want to end up in a brother ravine.

"That's good," Brown said.

"Imagine we'd have had to walk twenty miles back," Tom muttered.

— Shut up asshole don't be alarmist. Sorry, Emy, it won't happen again—Jean said with some sorrow.

8

— Not at all, don't worry, it's part of, besides, this is not an interstate highway. Don't you think? (laughs).

"Okay, now I'll be more careful.

Part 3

— I'm bored dad, are we going to get there yet? asked the youngest boy.

— Get to play your video game better Lucas. Hey Tom look at the map how far is left.

"Only fourteen kilometers. He responded sarcastically.

About thirty-five minutes passed in solitary landscapes full of tall trees and pines that gave an air of distrust in the depths of that nature. Luckily for the children who were already complaining for such a long journey; Two hundred meters away, a beautiful wooden house was spotted on the slope facing a small lake with crystalline waters. Jean then parked on top as there was no exact access to the abode which was about forty meters below rocky downhill geography.

"We're here at last, travel sucks when you can't smoke or hug a lady," Tom declared.

"Guys, put your things down, we'll leave the Van here," ordered Jean.

" Wow, what a beautiful view, I never would have imagined a place like this near our town," Emily said to Morgan.

Meanwhile, all the children ran meters ahead along with good Tom and his jokes.

"It will do them good Emily... you know these walks at their age are good, healthy coexistence" Jean commented while giving her a small smile.

— Thank you Jean, since I got divorced two years ago, we had not gone out to things like this, and believe me, I appreciate it very much,

— Don't worry, I do it from the heart, anyway, let's leave sentimentality, this place is to enjoy... let's go down, just lean on my shoulder because the ground is rocky and it's a bit steep and loose-.

It was one in the afternoon and the sun was reflecting on that beautiful Lake Waterland, the name of the place... Tom began to make a barbecue with chorizo and roast beef, all the adults drank craft beer and the children played in the crystalline waters of the lagoon,

"Naughty come eat now, I won't speak to you again," Tom yelled over a tiny hill on the shore of the lake.

"Here we go, Uncle Tom," a chorus of all was heard as they came out drenched in the water.

They all finished eating around two o'clock, and then took a two-hour nap.

"What a lovely evening, don't you think Tom," Emily stated.

-Yeah. And my brother I see that he is still sleeping apparently. I think he needs a woman to give him energy.

"Ha, don't say that, I didn't want to wake him up, he's tired, leave him alone!"

Why don't you declare to my brother? They both like each other, I know. Tom hinted.

"Enough, I don't feel right for a relationship right now."

-If you say so. In one of those they earn it for not speeding up the pace, then don't say I didn't warn you.

In that Tom turned to where all the children were sitting and proposed to them - hey lazy, I bring a ball, don't you want to play some football? Do you see that field without vegetation behind the house next to the trees of the forest?

Three of them said — sure Uncle Tom.

"So let's play, Emily do you want to play?"

" I'm still full, play, I'll stay watching the beautiful waters," Emily said as she looked into the distance at the panoramic view.

"Okay, you're missing it, that's why women always gain weight..." he murmured as he went to the back of the house with the rest of the kids.

— You two boys will kick first, Anita, you will be the goalkeeper on those two stones that I put, fine, and if they score a goal you will go for it, okay? - indicated the uncle.

"Okay," said the girl.

Sam went first and blew the ball away and had to go for it into a densely wooded area, then it was Jonathan's turn and goal.

— Lero lero Anita will have to go for the ball — they all shouted between laughs.

Not knowing exactly where it fell, the girl advanced because of the voices behind her that indicated that it was ahead, when she walked through some long-leaved pine trees surrounded by wild branches, she looked in the distance at the white ball near a vine, and when it was getting closer, approximately twenty meters from its objective: a man dressed as a scarecrow appeared with a long face with saw teeth that served as a mask, the girl remained motionless with her eyes wide open, the strange being shook its head and she took the ball, and then that saw-mouth opened and smiled, and slapped the ball at her, and it landed right at the girl's feet. The saw-mouthed man signaled with his finger for her to pick it up, she crouched down without losing her gaze, and immediately the reaper scarecrow went back behind some bushes, and that is when the girl ran terrified through the foliage ... when he arrived, everyone was asking him why he had taken so long. When Tom didn't answer, he asked her — are you okay, Anita?

Without saying a word, the girl pointed to the forest.

- What's up Anita? Did any animal you saw scare you?

This time he responded in a stuttering voice.

— A man with a mask over there. He pointed again towards the thick forest.

— A man with a mask? But," Tom exclaimed as he turned his gaze deep into that hilly vegetation.

— Most likely you were confused with the shadows girl, you are not used to seeing huge pine trees. Well, game over let's go back to the house.

"Because of you we won't play anymore," grumbled the children who ate her with their eyes.

At the same time Emily and Jean were talking sitting on the edge of the lake with a view of the sunset. They got along very well, and the friendship that started like this was gradually escalating to something more.

"You know Emily, I dare not tell you this, but, I would like to ask you, have you never, you know,

— Mom, — interrupted the smallest girl — mom Anita has been weird since we played soccer for a while, she didn't want to have a snack, she didn't even eat her favorite cake,

— Honey, wait a little bit, right now I'm going to finish...

- It's okay mommy. - Refuted the girl.

"Childhood stuff," Jean said, smiling at him.

"Would you mind if I leave you for a moment and go to...?"

— Of course not Emy, go ahead, go... maybe, seeing me here with you, you know, it's never the same to see your mother with someone else, although I suppose she senses it, and I anticipate it; We are nothing yet, but I enjoy your company.

"Thank you, how nice you are to me, I'll be back."

"Honey, why didn't you want to eat your favorite cake?"

- I'm not hungry.

- Are you feeling well my girl?

"Hey, Emily, since she went for the ball, she's been weird," Tom said, lying on his back on an old mattress in the background.

- And where did he go?

— It was a dynamic that the one who scored a goal had to go for the ball inside the trees of the forest — he explained.

Part 4

Turning back to Anita Emily asked once more.

— Honey, did you see any animals? Why are you like this? tell me with confidence.

— There was a man with an ugly mask behind the bush.

- That? How with a mask? In the middle of nowhere?

- Yeah.

" He said the same thing," said another of the children.

— Indeed, Emily, he said something like that, but most likely it was the shadow of the trees, I'm telling you because as children we used to see things like that, but in the end they were just illusions of the shadows of the branches.

"But the man threw the ball at me," the girl assured with obvious fear in her eyes.

- That? They all murmured at the same time as they looked at each other.

"And why didn't you tell me?" Tom said, getting up.

— And what do you think it is? Emily asked somewhat worried as she stared at him.

"It must be a prankster who was out there dabbling... look Emily!" It's safe here, why should you care? You have Jean an ex-military and also me, everything will be fine.

"Look, I'm worried about the safety of the girls, and then leave me, I'll go outside to tell Jean everything."

"Hey Jean," Brown yelled as he went up the wooden steps.

- What's up Emily? Everything is alright?

— I'm fine, but I don't like something.

— Tell me, what's going on?

— Well, a few hours ago while you were sleeping as I told you, everyone was playing futsal behind the house on the ground... the point is that my girl Anita went for a ball, I think about fifty meters in the woods , and when she came back she was like mute, that's what all the children said, just like your brother, and that's why he's like this, in short, I asked him why? and you know what she said: that a man in an ugly mask scared her in the woods and threw the ball at her and suddenly she disappeared. I'm not calm Jean when I hear that, I tell you; I won't feel comfortable sleeping in the middle of nowhere at night.

— I'm sure it wasn't a misunderstanding, shadows or animals are common here.

"No," he denied dryly, biting the corners of his lips.

— None of my girls are scared by seeing shadows, let's be honest... besides, Anita is not one of those girls who fears anything, it must be something strange for her to have become like that.

"Okay, we'll go. — answered Jean, — If you ask me, we'll leave right now, we already had fun, it's still 5 pm. we have about two hours until dark and we could easily hit the road before dark. Okay, let's pack everything up and get out of here.

After a few minutes, everyone was packing their luggage and things ready to put them in the car a few meters uphill. Jean and Tom were in the living room of the house.

— Whoa! the best part was tomorrow," Tom whispered annoyed.

"Calm down old man, Emy is right, it may be true and it may not be a crazy person the girl saw, but it's better to be calm for them... you know, there's no problem for me, but you know, I'm just giving this next step... and if she gets upset about my alpha male pride, you know, she won't trust me for future trips.

" Okay brother, let's go then."

In the room below everyone was waiting.

"Vacation's over," Tom joked as he threw a tennis ball at one of the boys that bounced off his head.

— Don't be an asshole man, it hurt.

— Tom closes the door, let's go, children already leave the house, uncle Tom is going to close.

After climbing the tiny mountainside something chilled them.

"Children of your... it can't be," Emy yelled hysterically.

"Who the fuck did this?" Thom countered, kicking the air.

- Good heavens! Someone punctured the tires," Jean exclaimed as she put her hands to her head, and immediately looked around in disbelief.

Emy began to shake next to the girls.

— I told them and they didn't believe me, Anita never lies, that crazy man surely struck them out, who else? - assured the mother.

"She's right, this isn't right," Jean argued as she opened a suitcase and took out a 9mm caliber pistol.

- Why are you armed? she asked a little annoyed.

— Don't worry Emmy, it's for security, as you well know I was in the military and I have permission to use them, also if any prankster tries to do that near the house they will receive a shot, rest assured. We don't have spare tires so tomorrow we'll walk to the highway, I think that right now it's a bit late and the night would catch us in the middle of the road; and that way would be risky.

"It can't be," Emy murmured as she clenched her teeth impotently.

"Mom, I'm scared," Anita said, "don't worry, honey, nothing's wrong.

"Let's go back inside the house, there's nothing to do here," ordered Jean.

Part 5

Once inside the house, he ordered his brother to close the door at the back and block it with some boards for safety, and in the front they put a heavy old armchair. They were all sitting in the living room drinking tea. The house only had one floor and two doors as access, with two windows at the front with a view of the lake; the most vulnerable part of the house in case someone breaks it, since there were no metal protections, there were only wooden rods stopping the window.

"Calm down Emy, everything will be fine, we'll leave early tomorrow," Jean told her as she hugged her tenderly. "Here we will all sleep together," he said.

— To all this, what do you think was what Anita looked at?

— I'll be honest, in my opinion he must have been a prankster, around here there are no towns, but bandits usually come, I mean, youngsters , you know, to do nonsense. It is my point of view, and since it was Halloween a week ago it is logical that they are still using them to scare.

— I remain calmer with your explanation, maybe that was it.

Gun in hand, Jean and company spent the night without incident. Early in the morning Tom was the first to wake up and open the door.

- That? que the fuck , what the hell is this book — he said to himself as he picked it up at his feet. — Uh, " *don't buy me* " what a shitty title, fuck jokers, - and then he stopped his finger in the direction of the lake. — This they will know, but first, well, what will this one say? book looks older than my ex, who didn't squeeze anymore.

Tom began to leaf through the book, and on the third page the same message was read, similar to the one that Anita had previously read to her mother two weeks before. When he finished reading it, he cursed the air as was his custom. - these sons of bitches want to scare with childishness, bah!, those who made this book only spent on empty pages -.

"Guys , get up , I have something to show you," he yelled at everyone while some of the children murmured because he had woken them up. Emy woke up instantly as did the girls.

— What's up brother, it's too early for jokes, don't you think? It's barely half past six in the morning

— It's not a joke Jean, just that the jokers or the joker left this book at the entrance of the wooden stairs right at the door.

- You're sure?

"I'm sure my name is Tom."

- What the hell? It can't be," Emily choked.

— What's up Emmy, are you okay? It's this book," Tom asked as he showed it closer to her.

"No, no," she murmured.

— Mom, it's the same book I read to you, remember? two weeks ago.

— Yes, honey, it's the same one and as far as I know you threw it in the trash, right? Anita.

—Yes mom I threw it away, but when I threw the book that time you also remember that I told you that I saw a man standing on the other side of the street right at the Hamilton house.

— Yes, but I had forgotten, and what was it like?

— Well, it looked like a scarecrow and had a mask somewhat similar to that of that man in the woods. Very similar to the photo in the book.

— I don't like this at all Jean, I don't believe in coincidences, but this exceeds my limit.

— Don't worry, it's already daylight, surely these are isolated cases... around this time of Halloween, obviously everyone wears their costumes. Well, right now we'll have some breakfast and we'll leave, then me and my brother will return to the truck.

" Okay, okay, we have to have breakfast now.

"Guys, get up," ordered Jean, "we have to have breakfast, we'll have to walk down the road to get to town."

There is no time to wash the dishes, come on, it is still early before the sun hits us hard. I was thinking that it is better to take the most important things in the backpacks, the rest of us stay here later, my brother and I will come, since it is too heavy to carry everything now.

"That sounds right to me," Emily said.

Once it was closed, they went out to the small patio that was opposite and there Jean gave some instructions.

—Guys, I know it's a prankster who's doing this, but it's better to be warned, if I and my brother had come, nothing would happen, but Emily is right; The safety of all of you comes first... I want you not to get separated, it's not long, maybe two hours to get to the road, so Lucas and Jonathan, stay close to me, and you two girls together with your mother. Tom don't forget the bat.

It was 8:30 in the morning when they all left for the same dusty road they had come from in the middle of that dark forest full of trees and tall pines.

"We look like the same guys from the Texas Chainsaw Massacre movie, don't you think, Jean?" I hope I don't end up with my guts out," Tom broke in jokingly.

—Don't say nonsense... girls already know how my brother is always with his silly jokes-.

After about ten uneventful kilometers the children complained that they were tired and wanted to rest. His father agreed and they stopped just below a leafy tree.

— Who will be those vandals who played a joke on us and spoiled our weekend? Tom pronounced somewhat annoyed. "Just let me give those rascals a hand and they'll remember their mother," he added.

"Calm down brother! surely they did that yesterday, it is evident that they have already left, undoubtedly they were adolescents of not more than eighteen years of age who found this area charming for their misdeeds.

"Hey guys, don't fight," Emily interrupted as she rested right on a rock with the girls.

— But it doesn't seem strange to them, that the house was closed without any sign of tampering or some object that they have stolen, — He added.

—Tom, you're right Emily, that's strange, from experience I know that vandals or lazy people usually do graffiti, break windows and steal, but the house was intact, it's the strangest thing.

"They must be civilized vandals, right Jean?" his brother teased as he grabbed the bat and yelled into the woods.

- Come on sons of bitches! get off your ass, come over here and I'll crack your skull, ha! They spoiled my precious weekend and they are still hiding, garbage.

The boys were already used to Uncle Tom's reckless and wavering temperament, but the girls not so much, for which reason Jean scolded her brother.

—Watch your words Tom there are ladies in front of you, be more courteous.

— Excuse me girls — he said — But these things usually annoy me, we better move on because the sun will rise soon. — he said while advancing with his bat resting it on his shoulder while he walked without concern and hummed the song: *'I imagined'* by John Lennon.

"Uncle Tom is right, let's move on or it will take forever."

Then, about five kilometers further on; a mangled deer carcass stopped their path. On the body, there were dozens of red-eyed crows that looked at them almost with a subliminal message on their foreheads as if telling them: "die intruders." Everyone was alerted even the incredulous Tom.

"My God, who did that?" Emily said instantly, blocking the smaller girl's view.

— Don't look at this, what the hell is that Jean, are there wolves here?

"We'd better keep moving forward, pass by," he said somewhat alarmed.

Part 6

— It doesn't stink yet, that means it's recent; maximum three hours. Tom pointed out.

— I don't like this at all, first about Anita, then about the book, what the hell is this? They're all over us, what the fuck, ever since the book came out... I don't like this at all," Emy said. "I don't even have a problem with anyone playing a joke like that on me, I don't even talk to the neighbors," he added.

"Maybe it's a coincidence, don't worry," Jean told her as she walked with her eyes straight ahead.

"Tom, how much longer?"

— I forgot the map, but I feel like about ten kilometers —he answered. — I see that the sun is already heating up, how good the shady part of the path is.

"The thing that interests me the least is the shadow Tom," Emily told him, a little upset.

Anita was walking with her mother on the left side with a view of the depths of the forest, on the other side was her younger sister. When they came to a turn in the road that was a little in the middle of some small mountains, ideal for ambush in those years of the old west... suddenly he managed to look camouflaged between semi-dry and greenish trees at the same man similar to a scarecrow with a strange sawtooth mask just like the one in the book drawing. He immediately poked his mother in the ribs, pointing up at her.

- What happen dear?

"Mom up, up, there it was.

"Well, what's going on back there?" — Jean said as she turned — what are you seeing above?

— The same man in the mama mask.

- That? It can't be — her mom murmured something upset.

Jean took out the baseless weapon at her waist and turned to face that direction right where some branches were moving due to the inertia of something that moved them.

— That bastard has already run... Tom, stay with the children, I'm going upstairs, that prankster is sure there, I'll teach him a lesson.

"Be careful," Emy told her as she hugged her two girls.

— Don't worry, I'll be right back, I'm used to these things. — Jean pronounced as she held her 9 mm weapon and climbed a battered and steep slope towards Mt.

Part 7

—Don't worry Emy, my brother was a military lieutenant, he knows what he's doing, he's also very good at shooting, it's not for nothing that he has several first places in target shooting. he confessed.

— It is that there are many coincidences, first a book that arrives at my house without my asking for it, then my daughter that day looks at the same guy in the face. At the time I didn't pay attention to it until now when my girl looked at it in the middle of the forest and it was the same... and worst of all, the book that we threw away appears in the middle of nowhere and at the door. And now a mutilated deer, ah! and forgot the most important thing; someone punctured all four tires of the car... and I think those jokes are a joke; it's over — She said something upset and nervous while biting her already dry lips from doing so much.

"You're right, don't worry, we're going to get to the road."

Meanwhile Jean in the middle of the tall longleaf pines, pointed his gun straight ahead, obviously with deadly military tactic, and yelled into the air.

—I don't know what your damn problem is, if you're here, show yourself, I'm not up to playing games... they had the audacity to puncture my tires, to scare my guests and you're still bothering us when we're about to leave this damn road, come on! uncle! Stop fucking son of a bitch, otherwise you're going to get shot.

When he finished saying those words, a noise behind him moved some branches, Jean immediately turned around and luckily it was just a coyote fleeing the place, but when he was about to return, the same man he had seen appeared in front of him. the girl , and wore an exaggeratedly baggy, scarecrow-like outfit, plus a saw-mouthed leather mask with no eyes, and huge worn-out black shoes with red laces, and in her hand was a spiked metal mallet . Jean looked at him in amazement, but his military training made him a bit cold-blooded, so he was not intimidated and took aim.

"Surely you're a bloody madman, but I warn you that this weapon I'm aiming at isn't a toy and it doesn't spit water, and if you take a step forward I'm going to fill your stomach with holes," he warned.

The strange scarecrow being stood still, but suddenly began to walk towards Jean. Without giving it much thought, the ex-soldier fired two projectiles at his legs, but realizing that they did not make a dent, he shot him three times in the chest, but it was not enough either, so he unloaded the entire charge, finally knocking him down.

Her adrenaline pumping, Jean briskly ran through the bushes back to the others.

"Run," he warned from afar.

What were those shots? Tom asked as he took one of the children by the hand.

"There's no time, but Anita was right, he's a fucking freak in a leather mask, run," Jean repeated as she loaded the last clip of the 9mm.

Seconds later when he caught up with everyone who was breathing hard.

- What the hell happened up there? Emy asked as she ran.

— There is a guy with a spiked weapon... he ate fifteen bullets, but I don't know if there are more with his hobbies, the fact is that he received fifteen bullets and still tried to get up.

— It can't be, I already said, a place like this in nothingness never brings anything good.

"Forgive me, it was never my intention."

Part8

After running for a while they stopped, since the children couldn't take it anymore.

— Don't worry, I still have fifteen bullets in case someone shows up. I don't think it was that guy, though," Jean asserted as she looked around the road.

"And what was that patient like?" asked his brother. When Jean was about to answer, a spiked mallet appeared from the middle of the trees and plunged into the vicious Tom's skull, leaving him inert and with an orgasmic grimace on his face. Immediately afterwards the same scarecrow with a saw-mouth mask appeared coming down the slope towards the road. They all turned around at the same time when they saw Tom's body lying on the ground like garbage... the girls and Emily screamed in terror while Jean tried to calm them down, but it was impossible, when they saw the thing that had killed her brother.

"I don't know if that thing is human or not, but it was shot fifteen times and should be battered." There's nothing in this world that can take that... I don't know what the hell it is, but he doesn't look hurt. I want you to run with all your might with the boys and girls, there are no more than three kilometers left, you can do it, I'll try to distract him as much as I can, I'll shoot the rest of the bullets.

— No. Don't do that Jean, we better run together there's a better chance that we'll make it out alive, that thing will catch up with us, come on! Do what I say.

"Please come with us," one of his sons murmured. 8

Hurry up, maybe I caught up ahead, come on! that thing is getting closer.

Emily and the rest ran with impetus until they lost themselves in the dirt road. Behind him twelve shots were heard and then a sepulchral silence spread behind him. After an exhausting twenty-five minutes they managed to get out of that sinister wooded place.

"Mommy, my feet hurt," Laurel was saying, as the older girl limped a little.

—"I'm afraid to say it, but that thing is the same as the one in the book", — Emily said to herself mentally, avoiding scaring her daughters at all costs, — "I'm afraid the curse is being fulfilled, I don't believe in magic, but, yes, it's true what the book says on that page, well it's nonsense I don't believe in that, most likely it is a crazy psychopath who spied on us or I don't know, but he tries to kill us "-.

About thirty meters away, he saw the interstate highway that led to the town, he crossed it along with all the children... in his hand he had a rosary and in a prayer position he implored in murmurs — let's go! a car, let a damn car pass...

After a few minutes, luckily for everyone, they saw in the distance a brown Volkswagen t2 type ambulance, perhaps from the forties.

-"My God! finally a car" — he said to himself.

When the car stopped Emily approached her and said almost in a pleading tone, but waiting for a bit of calm — could you give us a lift to the town ma'am, our car broke down, we were attacked in the woods, please, that crazy man must be close to the road.

"I'm very sorry," answered the old woman, about seventy years old. "Okay, you can get on, but clean your soles, I don't want dust," he added with a mean coldness.

—But before that I let you know that I'm not going to the town of Waterland or Wilstermann as you call it .

"Then where are you going?" - she asked a little surprised.

— I suppose you know the valley that is coming to your town.

—Of course we know it, that nursery is beautiful.

— Well, I'm going to collect some medicinal plants there.

"I understand, it doesn't matter if it takes us away from here, it would be perfect for us," Emily said a little hastily, turning around somewhat paranoid and imploring the old woman to start the fucking engine of that car that looked like a fossil.

—Sounds good to me, if that's the case, go ahead, then get on the back, this front door doesn't work. — He pointed out the old woman who appeared to be from another era because of her forties-type clothing.

After they hurriedly climbed in and got comfortable in that messy old car, he thanked:

— Thank you very much, ma'am, I'm Emily, the children belong to an acquaintance and the girls are my daughters, I thank you for your kindness in bringing us.

The white-haired old woman didn't say anything, just paid for the radio. What yes, is that he gave an unreliable appearance, coupled with his badge that he took out of his mouth as if it were a tic and put it impregnated with saliva. His sunken eyes were scary.

— And do you live near here? asked Mrs. Brown again.

"I live on the other side of your town, but I need some medicinal plants that can only be found where I go," the lady replied with an indescribable hoarse voice.

— And what is it called if I may know?

"My name doesn't matter," said the old woman, somewhat annoyed.

Emily, realizing the antipathy of the old woman, better stopped asking questions.

A few kilometers from reaching the dirt road that led right to the nursery, apparently the destination of the old woman, Emily realized something terrifying, something that she had not noticed when she got on and that was right in front of her when she asked for the raite ...on the old woman's board was the same book that had arrived in her post two weeks before, and the same book that had been put on the door of the cabin; **Don't buy me and on the cover a portrait of the man with a saw mask** , when he realized it was the same, a chill from the bottom of his soul ran through every pore of his skin, his throat went dry, and his hands began to shake. She couldn't explain why the hell this was happening to her, but inside she wondered: "What did that old woman have to do with the book? Or was he related to that madman in the woods?

It was obviously something he didn't want to find out. But that detail had made him terrified to imagine, obviously he couldn't get out of the car there in the middle of the road, because there were still at least ten kilometers from the nursery to the town, and if that old woman called, in the event of meeting that crazy person, they would be in trouble . . Undoubtedly, he had more questions than answers.

When she finally reached the dirt road, the mysterious old woman gave them the signal to get off because that was as far as it went, immediately afterwards Emily, very nervous, went down with the others. Without waiting for another car to come, he told the children to start running.

"Mom, why do we run?" asked the older one.

- Emily told him - on the board that old woman brought the same book that came to our house two weeks ago.

- But...

"I don't know, stop running."

They had not traveled more than a kilometer when the police car caught up with them and it was officer Torres, a veteran town sheriff.

"They're exercising," he said jokingly as the patrol wheeled past them. Emily, almost fainting, yelled at him:

— Help us! someone trying to hurt us, I don't know what the hell is going on.

Torres made a long face of disbelief.

"Here in Waterland , does anyone want to hurt them?" Well, I don't know what you've been doing, but, well, get in the car, and tell me what's going on.

After telling her everything in detail, Officer Torres seemed a bit touchy, and just in case he took them to town, and together with six officers by law they urged Emily to show them where Tom's "murder" occurred, and the whereabouts of Tom. Jean-.

Part 9

"You have to come with me, miss," Bailiff Torres said to her, who looked a little out of sorts.

— No again, I don't want to go there, you don't know what we spent there officer, that thing with a mask killed everyone and what happened to Jean, I don't want to go to that lonely forest again.

—There is no reason to fear, before notifying the higher authorities I have to make sure that it is true.

—But, I am telling you the truth, because you are not going alone.

"You have to do it by law Emily, it's part of the protocol." Besides, you don't have to be afraid; Seven more officers will go with me, all armed. We are going in three patrols. Boys and girls will be looked after by two policemen; they will be fine, we will not take more than two hours.

After Emily was convinced, the policemen traveled to the scene, the same disturbing road. Arriving at the beginning of the dirt road, Emily shuddered just going back into that place, but she had to. After thirty minutes they arrived at the same place that the woman had indicated, but there were no traces of blood or bodies, nor any sign of a massacre. Torres, thinking that it was all a misunderstanding, ordered the police to continue until they reached the lake and make sure of it definitively.

"Are you sure this was real, Miss Brown?" Torres asked in front of the lake house. -I hope it's true.

— Officer Torres we have known each other for years and he would never invent something like that, he knows it very well.

— I know you from my list, that you are a correct person, but, we have just checked and there is no body, the officers are already inside and they apparently do not see anything abnormal. I know Mr. Jean and Tom, surely they must be around.

"I'm not making anything up, damn it, understand," Emily asserted a little annoyed.

"That thing killed them, even Jean sacrificed herself so we could all escape down the road, and that's why she found us running."

"Sounds quite credible, but without evidence we can't do anything, miss, first we'll search the town and then alert," the officer said as he gave the order to everyone that it was time to go.

On their way back, officers found the trail blocked by two felled trees. The officers were alarmed as was Emily, and immediately from the top of the mountain they were ambushed by men dressed in scarecrows and Sierra-mouthed hoods.

On this side of Texas there is a rumor that these murderers still live among those mountains in the town of Wilstermann . The identity of that old woman was never known. According to what the girls told is what I tell in this story. But in theory, that old woman, perhaps she was the mother of the psychopath or psychopaths who inhabited or inhabit that part of that forest. If you get a one-page book with no content and the sawtooth face as the cover; don't read it, and throw it away. Anita's theory is that apparently the old woman is to blame for the disappearances of people in that place, because at the beginning of 1900 all those mountains were taken from her by foreign mines and originally Waterland . And because of that hatred, they made some books with the legend : *"don't buy me"*, since it alluded to their lands that were eventually bought by outsiders from there.

Contact with the author:

Part 10

Horror story

Tomas, a boy of barely 15 years old, was herding his grandfather Raul's pair of cows along those inscrutable and steep trails of Onish, a village in the east of Germany in 1850...

Tomas had grown up in that place, and he was not afraid to go out in the afternoons to run up the slopes. In that settlement in the forest there were only a dozen rudimentary huts, among them those of old grandfather Raúl and his wealthy wife, doña Candelaria...

The boy had grown up with them after his mother died "under strange" circumstances in a cabaret. Uncle Raul decided to leave Hanover where they lived after that event... he didn't want to be reminded of that city. So he took his wife and his four-year-old nephew and left for some acres of land that had been inherited decades earlier from his great-grandfather.

-In the background you could see the old man grumbling, struggling to light the stove where they used to prepare food.

That house was enormous, it was not for nothing that old Raul had spent the last few years building wooden houses in Munich, and in that forest there was plenty of wood. So he had built the house of his dreams. A large courtyard loomed all around, and chicken coops loomed everywhere....

-You took too long," said the old man, who was no more than seventy, but the passage of time was already visible....

-I'm sorry, Grandma, it's just that...

-It's nothing," he replied in a bitter tone as he continued to his credit with those unlit logs.

He used to hit Raul when he was younger, although at that age he only insulted him. The one he did hit at least once a week was his wife Candelaria, for reminding him of the past of how he knew her.

-Tomorrow you have to go early to get the oldest cow, I will sell it, we have no money, and we have to go on Saturday to buy groceries, the last cheeses were not sold, and we need money. Suddenly he shouted. Tomas nodded, and left with his grandmother who was looking behind her, fearful as always of how her husband would react.

-I'm sorry, Grandma Mati, Grandpa has been more angry than usual lately.

-He's grown too old, son, and you know how they tend to get... Come on! Come and eat, I'll prepare the peas you like so much.

Faithful to the order, the next day, the boy got up very early and walked all that long way to do what his grandmother had told him.

That old cow that his grandmother was going to sell was his best friend, he had taken her to pasture and had tidied her up for the last 8 years, and he didn't want to say anything to his uncle, but he didn't want to sell her.

-I'm so sorry my dear little friend yuyis, what was the cow's name - he told her while stroking her head... he didn't want her to turn into steaks at the market, but if she didn't do what he said, maybe a beating she would take, and obviously he had to take her.

-Well, I don't want to sell you yuyis," he said once again. Suddenly he turned to one side of the plain looking for the other two cows, which were having better luck for now, since they were younger, produced more milk and that translated into money. It was not unusual for them to be out of sight, since they always used to walk behind the trees in that area, but they did not usually go too far...

-Well, where are they," he whispered to himself. Then he called out the names again: invi, Tesita, where are the little cows? Usually they always responded with noises or bellows, but this time there was nothing, after repeated calls.

-Wait for me here Yuyis, keep eating, I'll go to that patch of trees, maybe it's there... where did these damned women go!

For the boy that was nothing unusual, other times he had spent up to an hour looking for them, so he was not at all worried, but when he reached that patch of trees and rough terrain, fear began to subtly invade him. On the trunks of the trees lay multiple splashes of dried blood, but in spite of that it looked frightening and with the play of shadows of that place; it gave him goose bumps, he was not nervous at all, but he did not like it at all.

For an instant in his mind he thought that maybe it was a pack of wolves, when that thought crossed his mind he looked at the ground and grabbed a wooden stick just in case. He was a little stiff with shock, he wanted to control himself, but he could not. He took a fleeting glance at where he had left Yuyis, but he was no longer there.

-What the hell Yuyis, I told you not to move," he whispered to himself.

-Cow doomed. After taking a breath and convincing himself that this had nothing to do with his cows, and that at most it was perhaps a wounded deer or a hunter from the settlement where they lived, although on second thought it was not typical, the only one who knew he had an old hunting rifle was Don Abundio, but he no longer used to hunt after being blinded in one eye, so after considering it, this did not seem logical to him.

He swallowed saliva and stood looking through the trees downhill. After minutes of not seeing anything strange around him, he decided to go down the other side of the patch of trees to look a bit in the gorges for cows, although this time he did it quietly. His fear had subsided, but he was afraid that in case a predator was lurking he would not draw attention to himself. He went with the stick in his hand, even though in all those years they had never had any problems with wolves, so he consoled himself in some way.

-That's a lot of blood, he whispered. -The coyotes that eat Abue Matilde's chickens usually leave blood behind, but that's too much, I don't think they're dogs... it's a little dry, but it was less than an hour ago, she thought.

As his feet crossed the dense vegetation downhill, suddenly something suddenly stopped his walk, and what he had in front of him was a gruesome scene. About 15 meters away, between some trees with few leaves, lay two cows completely destroyed, cut in half and their guts emptied, it was a gruesome act.

Tomas froze, his stick even fell out of his hand in shock. The boy swallowed saliva wetting his dry mouth. He squatted down and hid among the vegetation, only his head and a bit of his shoulders protruding from the semi-dry foliage.

-Holy God, what is that? Invi Tesita, what happened to them? -she whispered to herself as she tried to walk away, but it was impossible because of the slippery slope.

- They cut off their heads," he said between his lips.

- Damn wolves must have been them. I have to get out of here.

He took a panoramic look and jumped up, and with his hands immediately climbed uphill, until again, after a couple of minutes, he reached the patch of trees, and immediately ran down the weeping trying to see the Yuyis on all sides, who was nowhere to be seen.

-Where are you Yuyis? Yuyis," he whispered softly, trying not to raise his voice too much. - Where the hell did you go?

Determined to get the hell out of there, he suddenly looked at the side of the mountain path and saw his beloved Yuyis split in two as if he had been closed with a double-sleeved zipper. Like the ones that used to be used between two people to cut pieces of wood.

He began to tremble at the disturbing scene. Instinctively, he wanted to grab a stone, but there was none nearby, so he started to run with all his strength, and did not look back. What he was experiencing he thought was a nightmare. As he ran he pinched himself, but it was clearly not part of a bad dream.

... After about fifteen minutes he reached the stream. There he made a slight pause, because he felt his soul leaving him from exhaustion.

He glanced back, and again it provoked an incessant fear, as if he were being watched through the cracks in the bushes. Without taking off his pants as he used to do, he jumped into the river, because this was no time for such details. When he got out of that side, he somehow breathed a little more relief, however, he still had about two kilometers to go to reach the settlement of huts at least 40 meters away from each other, which at most consisted of about 13 huts.

He took a deep breath and picked up two large rocks, and started running again. Inside he felt as if something was following him or watching him from afar.

After running for about twenty minutes, he finally spotted the patch of boxes scattered all over that area, and he felt relieved, at least he had been able to get to safety, he said he knew what. Because he was sure of one thing, that whatever he did to those cows was not animals, because Tomas knew well that animals do not split a cow in two perfectly and without noise... easily, if it had been a pack of wolves it would have been scandalous, but he did not even hear a noise.

I knew perfectly well that whatever had killed grandma's cows were human, at least that's what I thought.

-There is Mr. Misael's house," he whispered to himself as he quickened his pace, since by this point he no longer had enough strength to run.

- Señor Misael," he shouted a couple more times from the patio door about five meters away from where the entrance door was.

-Mr. Misael.

After receiving no answer, he thought he was in the field and moved on to the next one about thirty-five meters away and no one came out either.

-I think they're all working....

Ah!" he exclaimed, before reaching the next house, and thought of Mr. Abundio, the hunter, an old man married to an old woman, and since he was blind, he didn't work. He wanted to ask him for advice or something before going to his grandfather Raul and explaining everything to him, because he was afraid of arriving like this.

-Mr. Abundio, Mr. Abundio, ma'am, are you there?

Since the old man's house in question had no gate to block the way, he felt confident in passing. He slowly crossed the courtyard to the front door, a large oak door that blocked the light with deerskin.

When he reached the door, he knocked about three times without stopping, and whispered the gentleman's name countless times.

-Mr. Abundio, Mr. Abundio, is anyone here?

After receiving no response, he dared to open the door. As he peeked inside he noticed that it was somewhat dark, as there was no light coming in unless the back door was open. And he had gone with them before to bring her cheeses, and he knew her when he closed the door behind him. He went to the kitchen and when he arrived, a macabre scene appeared again in front of him, among shadows and barely dazzling appeared the body of Mr. Abundio hanging, pierced from the back with a hook that came out of his throat. And above his head protruded a huge deer's head that the man had hunted years ago. On the table was the old wife of the party in pieces, and it was a scene straight out of Poe's worst horror story.

He could not explain the reason for all this. The poor boy thought he would soon wake up and come back to reality, but no matter how much he pinched himself and trembled, he did not come back.

And then, when he decided to turn to leave in panic, he stumbled over a sickle, and realized that whoever they were, they were probably men or outlaws from somewhere else, so he tried to get out of there, and ran and ran until he reached his grandparents' house, praying to the gods of Olympus or whatever he believed in, that his grandparents had not gone through the same thing, he would not forgive them.

Once he arrived, he took a thick stick and removed the lock from the door leading to the backyard. And he walked carefully to the entrance of the house. But what caught his attention in that strange morning, around eleven o'clock, was that the chickens were nowhere to be seen, nor the two dogs Lucas and Chombi, nor even the birds could be heard, it seemed that everything had disappeared. He swallowed saliva and before entering, he glanced behind his back just in case, and then he went inside...

When he set foot inside, he realized something scary, and that is that his grandparents had gone through the same atrocious experience on behalf of those damned psychopaths whoever they were, but unlike all the previous ones he looked at, the bodies of both, especially of grandfather Raul, were torn to pieces in a savage way, as if before having been cut into pieces: he had been vilely tortured, because his flesh was horribly black and crushed.... The only recognizable part was his head and his face without eyes, completely skinned.

At that moment he wondered what the poor grandfather had done to deserve so much, even if he had behaved badly with him, not even in his worst nightmares would he have done that to her. On the contrary, Grandma Matilde was only dismembered, and her womb pulled out by her noble parts, it was equally savage, and her head on the table.

Tomas at that moment was left without strength, he did not know what to do or where to run, because if he went out and went to the other houses that he was unable to go, he would surely find the same scene, therefore, he thought of hiding in the bush and fleeing from there to the town of Rakit about fifteen kilometers downhill.

And then darkness enveloped Tomas and he fell to the ground.

]

5 *hours later...*

Come on, wake up! Come on, wake up! -voices were heard inside a concrete room.

The boy barely opened his eyes, and realized that he was tied up, and in front of him a bunch of bearded, fierce-looking guys.

- Son of a bitch, they shouted at him while others spat at him.

Tomas stammered trying to get a couple of words out and ask them what he had done to deserve all that ordeal, and he was beaten for that point.

What did I do, sir? he asked the old man in front of him. A guy with a patch over one eye. Another younger man, about 50 years old, was smoking a cigarette, and the others he couldn't see, because they were out of reach of the only oil lamp that illuminated the area?

Suddenly the guy with the patch began to guffaw... And he said,————You know, when I was younger I always said I would take revenge on that bastard, and everything he owned.

Tomas did not understand what those words meant, it was that beyond the words, it was sometimes difficult to understand the Serbian accent they had, it was clearly not German but Serbian with a German accent. Again the boy answered almost on the verge of tears as if pleading not so much for his life but for the torture.

-I, sir, I am 15 years old..., I have done nothing in my life to deserve this, I only grazed my grandfather's cows....,

- Shut up," said the old man as he threw the still lit cigarette at him, and it hit his face leaving a light ash mark.

-Well, before I finish my revenge, I'll tell you a little," he said, then turned his back and sat down on a rudimentary chair. The other subject moved away from the light and remained in the shadows, just like the other subjects, only their huge silhouettes could be perceived.

"Thirty years ago the Bavarian army, of which your miserable grandfather was a member, tried to take over an area of the kingdom of Prussia, in those years we lived in the north, in a small farming region. I was a small businessman who gave a lot of work to the people..., that locality was beautiful, besides, we were all very united there, at the most we lived about two thousand people. Then, when a unit of the Bavarian army came in, they made abominations. After thoroughly investigating who was the culprit of those orders, we found out that it was an officer named Raul Vadover Kisok".

After finishing that, he swallowed saliva and remained silent for a few seconds. It seemed to hurt the sixty-five year old man greatly. Then he proceeded a little more calmly.

"We thought they would leave the women alive, but that was not enough, they raped them all together, and then they killed them. When finally the Prussian army expelled them and peace agreements were made for the cease fire, everybody forgot about it, but not us... we wanted revenge, and I Benjamin Ranke, a businessman, swore to myself that I would not die before I saw the revenge consummated, I spent all my savings at that time to investigate who they were, and you know? during the last thirty years we have been executing all those soldiers who participated in that battalion, the only one we had lost, the trail: it was the main bastard, and he was your damned grandfather..., he was the last one, number fifteen hundred of that unit. I swore to myself that all those who belonged to him would die. That's why the cows, and that's why everything about him. You can't imagine how much he suffered. But, unfortunately, we lost sight of you when we had you there in the plains. The ideal would have been for him to see your end in front of his eyes, but you can't always have everything. So, young man, here you go!". He exclaimed in an ironic tone.

At that moment Tomas understood something; that his uncle Raul had had a dark past that he had never imagined, and he knew that he had been a soldier and that. And that before his mother's death he had left his position as a shooting coach, but from being a simple low-ranking officer to a bloody murderer, that put him in a different type in his mind.

Old Benjamin got up slowly, then reached slowly into his trench coat, and immediately pulled out a strange blade. Tomas sensed the worst. He knew it was the end, and well deserved after hearing that dark story. And despite the fact that his uncle was a monster, without them as family figures and not knowing anything outside that place, he felt he had nothing to stay in this world, so he resigned himself to whatever was to come.

Benjamin walked towards him ready to finish him off. But then, the guy second in command surely, stopped him with these words: Listen Benjamin! the boy has nothing to do with it, let him go, if you want to appease a little your revenge, at least poke his eye out and let him go, it is not fair that for sinners pay saints.

Benjamin paused for a second and began to laugh out loud. And then he exclaimed.

-You think I'm going to let it go, Theodore. I spent the last thirty years savoring these moments of justice. And now you tell me: let him go. (Laughter again)

Benjamin began to take a few steps ready to cut the boy. Tomas said nothing. Then the guy behind Benjamin's back shouted loudly:

-Put your hands up Benjamin. I'm not going to be the same with him. We have already killed enough innocent people in this place for this boy to suffer the same fate. Teodoro pointed a single shot powder pistol at him. The other men next to him who were Benjamin's hired assassins did nothing to Benjamin's order to kill Teodoro, perhaps because they had earned Teodoro's respect.

-We are not going to make guilty of children. The ones we executed were great, but that's enough! You've already killed the main one, so stop it now!

- Is this how you repay me, Teodoro? Don't forget that I took you off the streets, remember?

Theodore looked down slightly, but did not allow himself to be manipulated, and again put his finger on the trigger.

-I said stop," he shouted again, this time more determined.

Then, all of a sudden, Benjamin spun around ready to throw the dagger at Teodoro, and just at that moment he received a shot in the chest that left him dead instantly.

Then he approached the boy with the dagger untied him and said:

Go on, go! No one will do anything to you... You can go.

The boy, as best he could, went down the stairs of that room and went out, clearly he did not know that modern city, but it seemed that they were in Berlin?

End

"Whatever you can imagine, it exists in the shadows. There is no limit to terror, no end to evil. In the darkness, the unthinkable comes to life and feeds on our deepest fears."

Thank you
Story added Story added

2023
Aiden Ziff

If you liked the story you can leave me a comment.

Terror Quote

"In the shadow of night, where reason fades and fear becomes a companion, the whispers of the unknown awaken the deepest fears of our existence. In the dark corners hide secrets that tear reality apart, while darkness feeds on our souls with inhuman voracity. Terror does not wait in the shadows, but is born from our own imagination, weaving nightmares that lurk in the folds of our mind."

Quote 2 of terror

"In the stillness of an ancient cemetery forgotten by time, the tombstones lie in silence as witnesses of a dark past. Amid whispers of sepulchral wind, an ancestral shadow awakens from its eternal lethargy. The twisted trees shudder, the fallen leaves dance to the rhythm of the macabre. Death takes shape, gliding among the tombs, its empty eyes searching for unwary souls. The trembling ground exhales a dismal sigh, and in an instant, lost souls emerge from their graves, eager for revenge. In the darkest night, under the blanket of the dying stars, the cemetery comes to life, transforming itself into a hellish stage where death claims its tribute."